Good Night God

Holly Bea

Illustrated by Kim Howard

H J Kramer
Starseed Press
Tiburon, California

Art Director: Linda Kramer
Design: Assumpta Curry, Tiburon, California
Production: Jan Phillips, San Anselmo, California

Special thanks to Brenda Knight

Library of Congress Cataloging-in-Publication Data

Bea, Holly, 1956–
    Good night, God / Holly Bea ; illustrated by Kim Howard.
        p.   cm.
    Summary: A child says good night to the house, moon, mouse, teddy
bear, Mommy and Daddy, and God.
    ISBN 0-915811-84-7
    [1. Bedtime Fiction. 2. God Fiction. 3. Stories in rhyme.]
I. Howard, Kim, ill. II. Title
PZ8.3.B3485go   2000
[E]—dc21   99-11014
                                                         CIP

H J Kramer Inc
Starseed Press
P.O. Box 1082
Tiburon, CA 94920
Printed in Singapore
10 9 8 7 6 5 4 3 2

For Steve, whose love, support, understanding,
and laughter make it all possible.
H. B.

For Reverend Douglas Huneke
of the Tiburon Westminster Presbyterian Church
for his thirty years of service and guidance.
K. H.

Good night, God, the day is done.
Good night, birds. Good night, sun.

Good night to the sky above.

Good night to the squirrels I love.

Good night, God, the moon is here.

Good night, trees, and good night, deer.

Good night, garden. Good night, house.

Good night to the little mouse
Who lives beneath the bottom stair.

Good night, kitties, waiting there.

Good night, Teddy, one, two, three.

Good night, angel, guarding me.

Good night, God, it's time for bed.
My daddy calls me Sleepyhead.

Mommy likes to hug me tight,
And listens while I say good night.

Good night, God, sweet dreams to you,
Tomorrow there's so much to do.

But now it's time to sleep and dream
Of rocket ships and fairy queens.

So thank you, God, for all you do,
And don't forget that I love you.

Good night, God.